SILLY BIMBO VOLUME 3

A BIMBO TRANSFORMATION ANTHOLOGY

SADIE THATCHER

CONTENTS

INTRODUCTION

This is an anthology collection of multiple stories that are too short to publish as standalone books. But each story still has heart and a sexiness that I don't want to deny you, the reader.

Thank you for reading this anthology book.

~ Sadie

A BIMBO IN MY HEAD

I'm not crazy. At least that's what everyone tells me. But not everyone has a bimbo in their head, constantly commenting on everything I do.

This is boring. Can't we do something fun?

That's what I hear while I'm at work. I can just be sitting there at my desk, going through my normal work routine, but even as I work as efficiently as I can, earning my monthly paycheck, I have a constant chatter going on in my head. Nothing I've ever been able to do has stopped it or even lessened it.

I call the voice in my head Bambi. All she ever wants to do is dress up in sexy clothes, go shopping during the day, and then go clubbing at night. If she had it her way, I would find ways to persuade men to pay for my lifestyle, making me a sugar baby to multiple men. Never mind the fact that I am a fully capable adult with a college degree and a job that pays me well enough that I've almost saved enough money to buy a house for myself.

And before I go into any more detail, I want to make it clear that I have seen doctors and therapists. At first no one believed me, but once I finally connected to the right kind of help, it turned out there was nothing they could do for me. I've been put on various antipsychotic medications, but nothing worked. Bambi was always there, commenting on my life, giving me the rundown on how I wasn't being sexy enough or simply distracting me from my intended actions.

With no luck in ridding my mind of Bambi, the doctors gave up on me. At least I don't have to be medicated anymore. I was in the same situation no matter what I did. Bambi was always there inside my head. I just have had to grin and bear it. And despite a few times when I've done something silly, getting distracted by Bambi's comments, I've mostly managed to maintain a normal life. It's just a different life than what every other person seems to live. It's like there are two people in my head instead of one.

Life with Bambi in my head is probably the worst at work. All Bambi wants to do is do the things she has termed as fun. And so while I toil away at my desk, doing both complex and mundane tasks for that paycheck, Bambi gives me an onslaught of complaints and comments.

I want to do some online shopping. Instead of being boring, you should look at pretty shoes to buy.

"Not right now," I will argue back. It's weird, but I can actually have conversations with Bambi. She is usually a chatterbox, but occasionally I can get her to shut up long enough for me to do something important. Unfortunately, that silence never lasts for long. She has the attention span of a gnat, so it usually doesn't take long for her to forget that there was a reason for her silence.

The worst part is when I'm in a meeting. First Bambi will comment about the men in the meeting.

Do you think he has a big cock? I bet he does. I would just love to wrap my lips around his cock.

Then once everyone is seated and the men's cocks, previously hidden behind slacks and trousers, are no longer within line of sight, Bambi finds other ways to try to sabotage me. She sings vapid pop songs. I don't even know where she knows them from, because I predominantly listen to classic rock music. But regardless of where she gets her music inspiration from, it's distracting.

The number of times I've started tapping my foot or nodding my head to the beat of whatever song she is singing is more than I want to admit. Her songs are distracting to the point where I sometimes zone out and miss large chunks of meetings. Her actions have definitely hurt my upward mobility within the company. My work is still good, but the impression I give others is sometimes lacking, mostly due to her intrusions into my encounters with my coworkers and bosses.

However, Bambi doesn't just come out during work. She is ever present in my mind and there is nothing I can do to fully make her be quiet. Going to see a movie in the theater usually means having to put up with her chattering away about how hot the men in the movie are or complain about the fashion of the women. And that's not when she's describing the plot as boring and how she wishes the main characters would just fuck already.

You like such boring movies. I want to pick the next movie we watch.

I have actually done that before. I had just finished college and I finally felt free enough to let Bambi out for a few hours. I figured watching a movie couldn't cause any problems. It turned out, however, that what Bambi really wanted to watch was porn. It wasn't even good porn. Her favorite adult movies involved over-inflated bimbos with more plastic than brains getting what was left of their minds fucked out by some ripped stud with the cock the size of the woman's forearm. Sure, it was hot, but it lacked the complexity I preferred in movies, even adult ones.

As one might imagine, with Bambi as a constant companion, I'm not the most social of people. I have a few friends, but I have learned not to share that I seem to have a second person inside my head. I tried that once and I'm not friends with that person anymore. They thought I was crazy. I tried to explain, but they couldn't comprehend it. No one seems to be able to grasp that I seem to have a second consciousness inside of me, someone with their own thoughts and feelings. Unfortunately, that sort of thing doesn't show up on a brain scan.

That isn't to say that I have been able to completely ignore Bambi's influences. Her suggestions tend to hold more sway when I'm tired or incredibly relaxed. One time, immediately after getting a massage, she managed to take me shopping. Short dresses, high heels, and loads of makeup were all added to my credit card bill that month. It took three months to pay it all off.

I do have to admit, Bambi has pretty great style, although it's mostly inappropriate for anything except clubbing. But I have been able to wear a few of those outfits on dates when I wanted to look extra sexy. I even let Bambi help with my makeup. I usually don't wear much so I don't have much in the way of skill. I honestly don't understand how Bambi has become so proficient with it, but I at least looked amazing on those dates.

Unfortunately, Bambi had a tendency to try and intercede during the dates. She would chatter vapidly about whatever came to mind, clearly trying to distract me. I think she was trying to make me look more like a bimbo. It certainly worked to a degree. But even when the guy was into that sort of thing, there was no way I was going to just jump into bed with him. Bambi's thoughts turned to sex so easily. I didn't understand how her brain could work that way.

That's not saying I'm a prude when it comes to sex. And there were a few times when I let her pressure me into sleeping with a guy before it felt right in the relationship. It was never bad sex. With Bambi along for the ride, she always seemed to make it feel good. I always came and always at the right time. But sex wasn't enough to build a relationship on. I needed more and each time I let Bambi pressure me into it, the relationship fizzled after that.

I knew that if Bambi was always in charge, she would be a constant partier. A night she was not getting fucked by some guy she just met or one of the guys she was playing sugar baby for was a night wasted. It was just how she thought. Or at least that was how I assumed she thought. We did not share thoughts specifically. We could talk to each other in my head, but that was separate from sharing our thoughts. That was always the part that most confused the doctors and therapists.

However, as much as I complain about Bambi, she has been fun at times. It was her suggestion that I go to Hawaii for my last vacation. I had a great time and I know she enjoyed the time I spent laying out on the beach in the sun. I returned with a nice tan after that and even got asked out on a date. James was a nice guy, but after a few dates it became clear that he wasn't the kind of man for me. I needed someone more intellectual, although I know Bambi thought he was nearly perfect. He certainly looked that way.

Sometimes I wish it was possible to give Bambi control for a night. The idea of letting her take complete charge and not just give me constant suggestions would be nice, because I think it would get her off my back sometimes. Instead, I have to listen to her the whole time.

But those suggestions do wear me down sometimes. I

rarely give her the opportunity to hold real sway over me, but over time there have been a few changes in my life that she has been the creator of. Most of those things have to do with my appearance, both in how I present my body and the clothes I wear.

It all started in college. I was away from home for the first time and Bambi kept getting in my ear. She was sneaky, telling me about how all the other women at school wore thongs. I wanted to fit in so I started wearing thongs. It turns out Bambi was either wrong, which was definitely possible, or she lied to me. Either way, I had grown so used to wearing them, that I always do now. I don't own any other kind of panties.

And it was also under Bambi's advisement that I got my belly-button pierced. If it were up to her, I would probably end up wearing low rise pants and shorts with a crop top of some sort on my days off. At least through Bambi's encouragement, I'm fit and trim, so it wouldn't be the end of the world if I dressed that way. I have the body for it.

That is one advantage to having Bambi along for the ride. She's really good at policing my diet and making sure I workout regularly. That's not to say I never splurge, but I definitely have the healthiest diet of my small circle of friends. I also spend more time working out every week than they do. But I have to say the results are well worth it. Sure, my boobs aren't as big as they could be, much to Bambi's complaint, but I feel more confident than I would without the workouts.

Bambi has more than once suggested that I should get a boob job.

Why have tiny tits when you can have big, sexy boobs?

Her suggestions never vary that much, but she always finds different ways of proposing it. And I can't say I've never been tempted. I'm sure Bambi and I have very different ideas of what big, sexy boobs are, but it's not like I couldn't afford them. I just haven't had a good enough reason to go through with it before. I was happy with my body, but there were times when I felt lacking.

Look at her. Doesn't she have a great rack? We could have boobs like that if you wanted.

Bambi gave me a regular run down of what she thought of other women and their boobs. Bambi could see out of my eyes, but she seemed able to view what I saw as if she were watching on a television screen. She could pick out details I had completely missed. I mostly ignored other people, but Bambi was able to pick out fellow bimbos with ease. And once Bambi started talking about them, I usually found myself looking more closely, trying to see what she saw. It was just natural, even if I wanted to remain focused on something or someone else.

But then I met Neil. Right away, I knew he was different from all the other men I had tried dating. He was handsome in a way that Bambi definitely approved of, but he was also incredibly intelligent. I had met many men who played at being intelligent, but I could tell right away that Neil was the genuine article. He just had an amazing aura around him. His presence was commanding and yet gentle, the perfect combination in my opinion.

Not that I was going to tell him about Bambi. Not yet, at any rate. But the comfort I felt with him was amazing. And for the first time in my life, Bambi approved. She had nothing bad to say about the man. Yes, Bambi wanted me to instantly sleep with him, but there was a significant difference this time. I wanted to sleep with Neil. But where Bambi wanted to sleep with him on the first date, I managed to hold off until the third date. For me, that was really soon, but it just seemed to fit.

And when it came to sex, Neil simply rocked my world. I

never knew sex could feel that good. Bambi did, but she was just as happy as I was. She was happier even, because once we broke the dam, Neil and I couldn't get enough of each other. He'd arrive at my place to pick me up for dinner, but I'd drag him inside and suck his cock. I let Bambi direct me for that, but she was amazing. And Neil clearly enjoyed our actions, because he was eager to continue the fun when we returned from dinner.

As our relationship continued to grow, Bambi's influence over me grew more and more. It was easier to let her take charge when I received so much pleasure back from Neil. And I could tell that he enjoyed some of my bimbo moments. The way his eyes lit up whenever I did something extra sexy or came across as less intelligent than I really was always made me secretly squirm in pleasure.

Men like Neil love hot and dumb girls like us. I bet he'd take really good care of us if you just gave in and went full bimbo.

I wasn't so sure about that, but I wasn't about to argue. Not now, at least. I had seen too much from him to fight back against Bambi's influences entirely. She was good for some parts of life for sure. She had a great sense of fashion and her knowledge when it came to sex could not be surpassed.

But then, three months into the relationship, Neil opened up to me. "I have a bimbo fetish," he had explained. He seemed nervous about it as he said it. He was opening himself up to me in a way he never had before.

As soon as those words escaped his mouth, I realized it should have been obvious from the start. The way he lit up whenever I gave into Bambi and her bimbo instincts, whenever I came across as dumb and overtly slutty, should have been a major cue. But now it all made sense.

"I can explain it all if you want, but I want you to become my bimbo."

Every word after that was meaningless. Neil kept talking, trying to explain himself, trying to explain to me what he meant, but I already knew. Bambi had been ready for this moment ever since she first appeared in my head. And to be honest, I was ready for this moment too. There was a part of me that wanted to give in and let Bambi take over, to become the bimbo she wanted me to be. And now it seemed that Neil wanted that too.

"I want to be your bimbo," I finally blurted out, more to stop Neil from burying us both beneath a pile of explanations that I was never going to listen to.

After that, life got a lot easier. I quit my job and moved in with Neil. He was adamant about taking care of all the details of my life. All I had to do was focus on looking pretty and pleasing him in the bedroom. But the bedroom was not enough. With all of my energy that I had once put into my job, I could not restrain myself from keeping the sexual side of myself in the bedroom. Before I knew it, I was doing everything I could to seduce Neil out in public.

My outfits pushed the boundaries of what was acceptable, my makeup lacked any subtlety, and when Neil offered to pay for breast implants, I jumped at the offer. Before I knew it, I looked how I assumed Bambi always wanted me to look. She was the impetus behind many of my changes, the catalyst for me becoming the bimbo that Neil wanted me to be. But more important than that, I was becoming the bimbo that I wanted to be.

And it reached a point where there was no longer any difference between Bambi and me. Sure, I was technically still a smart and capable woman, but no one looking at me or interacting with me would believe that I held any advanced degrees or that I had been anything other than a bimbo all my life. I actually liked the way people, especially other women, looked down on me, as if I was someone to be pitied rather than celebrated.

But the big moment came when Neil suggested I change my name. He had been calling me Bambi since he made his offer to me to become his bimbo. I let him know that I already had a bimbo side to me. I never told him about Bambi, but now it doesn't matter. I don't hear Bambi in my head anymore. We are one and the same. We are finally whole, a single person, a single bimbo living her best life.

I don't know what would have happened if Neil had never come into my life, but I was pretty sure I wouldn't be called Bambi now. Odds are probably decent that I would have gone over the deep end and ended up in a mental health facility that would lock me away. Not that I think about those things anymore. I don't think about most things. I'm not dumb, but I'm pretty sure my brain has atrophied since I gave up control to Neil. He makes my life amazing and I do everything I can to make his life amazing in return. The only difference is he cares for me and I make sure to give him every pleasure a bimbo like me can provide.

I'm not crazy, I'm just a bimbo. And I love it.

A WISH UPON A SHOOTING STAR

A shooting star streaked across the sky. Greta saw it and made her wish.

"I wish Angie a perfect life."

It was a simple wish and one that Greta never anticipated would come true. But it also spoke to Greta's selfless nature, wishing for others instead of herself.

Angie was Greta's best friend. They met on the first day of their university orientation and had been besties ever since. However, Angie had been going through a hard time recently. Her boyfriend broke up with her, after she caught him cheating on her, and she lost her job. Despite the hot labor market, Angie was having a horrible time finding a new job. She spent day after day, sending out resumes and job applications, but all she got back were rejection letters. She was depressed and the once ever-present smile on her face was now gone.

And so knowing her friend was in such dire straits, Greta wished for her friend to have a better life. But not just a better life, a perfect life. Greta wished that Angie could have a perfect life.

Angie, meanwhile, was about a mile away, fast asleep in her bed as Greta made her wish. She had exhausted herself with a mother batch of job applications. Each one got a custom cover letter. Angie wanted to stand out as best as she could and she knew that directly addressing the job she was applying for and the company she was applying to was her best shot at standing out. But all that energy spent on her applications drained her, leaving her to fall asleep far earlier than was normal for her.

But as Angie slept, a pink glowing light entered her apartment through the window. It was a light that originated from the shooting star that Greta had wished upon. The pink glow filled the room, leaving no corner or crevice dark. Then as Angie slept, her body began to change.

Angie had always had a plain appearance. Her light brown hair always had a stringy feel to it, so she kept it short and often put it up in a bun on the top of her head. However, while she slept, she let it flow freely across the pillow. But the pink light changed all of that. An outside observer might have guessed that it was a trick of the light, but it was all real. Angie's hair changed color, lightening until she sported a golden mane of hair, long and blonde, with enough volume and amazing silkiness to make the majority of women in the world jealous.

Next came Angie's body. Her pale skin darkened as a tan crept across her body. Every blemish she had, which included multiple acne scars from her younger days, simply disappeared. Between her hair and her skin, she now looked almost like an entirely different person.

However, Greta had wished for a perfect life for Angie, and that meant changing every part of her to reach perfection. Next came Angie's muscles. She had always been weak. She lacked the conditioning necessary to maintain her strong performance in gym class. She barely passed, with much of her grade dependent on her ability to complete athletic tasks. Now, however, her body grew sleek and toned, her waist shrinking and the inches melting away.

The greater fitness and tone of her body created a base from which the rest of the physical changes could be made. Long lashes appeared that would frame Angie's eyes. Her lips plumped up with such projection that they would forever draw the eye and men all over would imagine what those lips would feel like wrapped around their cocks.

But that was all assuming people could tear their eyes away from Angie's tits. They grew big and round, clearly fake, clearly the result of surgery. And those tits were complemented by an equally impressive bubble butt that would threaten the seams on almost any pair of pants or shorts. Even skirts would be put under pressure.

But it was not enough to just change Angie's body. She looked the part of a bimbo now with her ultra-feminine appearance, but she was still the same boring Angie on the inside. That was what changed next. The pink glow penetrated Angie's head, cleaning away all those pesky thoughts and worries that previously bogged down Angie's mind. At first, Angie's dreams simply vanished, but that did not last for long. Soon they were replaced with sexy dreams, images and scenarios of Angie's new form sucking and fucking in a nonstop orgy of debauchery.

Angie started to toss and turn, her long-nailed fingers pressing into her skin, her hands traveling down her body to the junction between her legs where she pressed against her clit and pussy, her body even convulsing as she came, over and over again. Her body shook with orgasm and a smile crept across her features. And all the while she slept as if nothing had happened or continued to happen.

But it was not enough to just create a new Angie in body and mind. Her whole life needed to be rewritten to match her new form. Angie's life as a studious and hard working woman was erased. Instead, her role in life had been transformed, becoming a creature of pure sexuality that she wore openly. Angie's closet emptied and then refilled with all sorts of sexy outfits. Tight and revealing were the primary themes. Her shoe collection exploded with more pairs of high heels than she could now count. Her wardrobe was slutty and sexy, but so was the new Angie.

The pink glow filled Angie's apartment, recreating it in her new bimbo image. Pink became a dominant theme. So too were the posters of scantily clad men and women. The new Angie devoted to femininity and the sexual experience. Her body was a work of art and her apartment highlighted that fact. Her furniture transformed, becoming modern and chic. Her bed grew in size and the sheets covering her shifted from cotton to silk.

When Angie finally awoke the next morning, her new mind booted up as if she were a brand new computer. Her eyes scanned the room as she sat up, letting the silky soft bedding fall from her enhanced features. Her lashes fluttered as she took everything in, noting the pink walls and the pink bedding. One look at her pink nails made it abundantly clear what Angie's favorite color was now. And pink looked great against her tanned skin.

"Where am I?" Angie asked as she tried to place herself. Her memories were hazy and there were still a few lingering shadows of her past life hanging at the periphery of her mind. But as soon as that question was asked, Angie jumped at the realization of how she sounded. Her voice was soft and higher pitched. It was like she was cooing to a baby, but it was simply how she spoke now, an extra change from Greta's wish.

But even the worry about her voice was soon replaced by an interest in her tits. The little jump she made was enough to get them to bounce slightly on her chest. Angie reached up and grabbed her tits, fully enjoying the way they felt in her hands and the way her hands felt on them. Angie's thoughts immediately turned sexual. If there was a moment where she was truly going to question her new reality, this would have been it, but she was lost to the pleasure she could provide herself.

Soon Angie was laying back again as her hands ran over her smooth body. Every inch of her was charged with erotic energy. When her fingers found her pussy and her clit, it felt as if fireworks were going off inside her head. She saw stars and rainbows as her eyes rolled up into the back of her head.

It only took moments before Angie's fingers completed their task, sending an orgasm like she had never experienced before roaring through her body. Wave after wave of pleasure flowed through her. But that first orgasm was nowhere near enough to fully satisfy the bimbo. She kept fingering herself right through to two more orgasms, never once stopping to actually sit back and ride the wave of ecstasy. But that was Angie's life now. She was a sexual creature and she could always make the best of every moment.

When Angie finally got up, she by then had realized that she was in her apartment. Whatever shadows of her past had been successfully ignored, leaving her clear on who and what she was. Angie knew she was a bimbo. She knew her mind could only handle the most simple of tasks. Her body had been sculpted through a combination of workouts and surgery to become the ideal feminine form, a perfect body. And thanks to Greta's wish, Angie now had a perfect life too.

It took several hours for Angie to get ready. She had slept in the nude, the pajamas she had worn going to bed the night before disappearing in her sleep. Now, however, Angie owned no pajamas, unless one counted the lingerie she owned that could act as sleepwear. But Angie preferred to sleep in the nude. It gave her hands space to roam on her body and it allowed her to enjoy the feeling of the silk sheets sliding across her perfectly smooth skin.

Angie first had to shower. She found a fake cock sticking off the wall of her shower with a suction cup. As she lathered her body with soap and cleaned herself, pushed herself back against the wall, filling herself with the fake cock. It was another two orgasms before she finished her shower, making for five so far since she had awoken, not that Angie was counting. For her, numbers were a mostly abstract device. They held little meaning for her. Usually they just swam in front of her eyes if she tried to focus on them for too long. Instead, she just ignored them whenever possible.

The shower finished with Angie dropping to her knees and licking the wall cock clean. She loved the taste of herself, especially as she pushed the cock deep into her throat. There was no gag reflex to stop her.

Once out of the shower, Angie spent most of the next hour doing her hair and makeup. The Angie of old had little understanding of what to do when it came to hair and makeup. The new bimbo Angie was an expert. She worked with surprising efficiency, but it still took a long time. When it came to beauty, Angie was a perfectionist. Plus, she had enough hair that it took time to properly dry and style. Her long nails did not help matters either, slowing her down as she added every bit of color to her face.

When Angie stepped out of the bathroom, she did so still naked, but her face now perfectly made up for a day out, or more like a night out. Angie's style had changed dramatically. Gone was the effort to downplay her features. Now Angie wanted to enhance her features. And when it came to her face, nothing was more important than enhancing her already full lips. They were covered in pink, matching the color of her nails, as well as her eyeshadow.

Angie stepped in front of her closet to try and decide on an outfit to wear. There was nothing there that could be considered modest. The new Angie ignored modesty. She always went for downright sexy. If she was not getting called a slut on a daily basis for her clothing choices, Angie felt as if she was being a prude. Then again, this new Angie was a slut. Sex for her was like a drug she could not quit. Her addiction had taken her fully, but she embraced it, loving how it made her feel. The chase, the act, the recovery were all a part of her life and she lived for that.

Angie eventually settled on a blue dress that stretched over her features, making it clear that she wore nothing underneath. The dress had laced across the chest, showcasing the largeness and roundness of her tits. The neckline was almost wide enough to reveal her nipples, but they were just barely covered, maintaining that part of her decency. The dress was short enough, however, that it would not be long before someone confirmed the fact she was not wearing panties. But in Angie's mind, panties would just get in the way. She avoided them whenever possible, instead preferring the ability to just bend over and let a guy thrust his cock into her from behind.

The final part of Angie's outfit were the heels she slipped her feet into. Her feet molded perfectly to the shape of the elevated heel, as if she had been wearing such shoes all her life. It certainly seemed that way with how well she was able to move in them. It was as if she were a dancer in high heels. Her legs actually felt better, more relaxed, once she donned the heels. Her body was made to be shown off in such shoes and she was well-adapted to moving in them without issue.

When Angie left her apartment, she did so with her tits bounding slightly in front of her and her long blonde hair flowing out behind her. Her ass and hips swayed back and forth with each step, giving people something to look at even when she was walking away from them. Her body was perfect from every single angle and it was clear what she had been designed for.

However, Angie was not on the hunt for cock as she left her apartment that day. That was her usual task. She jumped around between men, happily fucking around, especially when the men she favored helped to fund her lifestyle of sexy outfits and frequent trips to sunny locations where she could wear a bevy of bikinis and other revealing outfits. And despite all the skin she put on display, she never seemed to get taglines, another bonus of the wish that Greta had made for her.

This time, Angie was scheduled to meet with her friend. Greta and Angie had a standing weekly meetup over lunch. It had started when Angie first lost her job, but it had become a regular occurrence in her time spent hunting. Now, however, Angie hunted for something else. There were few jobs where she could be employed for long and even those she could work were too complicated for her to keep track of. Even stripping was too much for her. Angie really was just a fucktoy for men, but she would not have it any other way. For her, this was how she was supposed to be and how she lived her best life, her perfect life.

"Hi, Greta," Angie cooed when she walked up to Greta at the cafe.

Greta's eyes widened as she tried to take in all of the bimbo before her. Greta had arrived early. That was normal, even with the old Angie as her friend. She took in the new Angie, but her mind could not comprehend what she was seeing. There was no way that this bimbo was Angie. Greta had wished for Angie to have a perfect life, but this was not what she meant. She did not even expect the wish to come true. It made no sense.

"Angie?" Greta asked. Even as her mind grappled with

who this slut of a woman could be, she could only think of Angie, her friend. Only this was not the Angie she remembered. This was a completely different Angie.

"Of course, silly," Angie said with a giggle. She swung her ass into the seat opposite Greta and placed her long-nailed fingers on the edge of the table. "I'm so glad to see you. It feels like it's been forever."

Greta did not know how to respond to her friend. All she seemed capable of doing was staring into Angie's exposed cleavage. Those tits pulled in her gaze and locked it there. Greta had never experienced anything like it before.

"What happened to you?" Greta finally managed to ask, although she was definitely asking Angie's tits as opposed to her face. However, the new Angie was used to people talking to her tits. Half the time she had a video call, she managed to put her tits in the middle of the screen and was lucky if her lips were in view as well. It was how Angie operated now and she considered it completely normal. It was all she knew now.

"What do you, like, mean?" Angie asked. "Did I dress bad or something?"

Angie's poor grammar shocked Greta out of staring at her tits, but looking up did not help her eyes from looking like wide saucers. The surprise and confusion over the person Angie had become was too much for Greta. She felt completely overwhelmed by the vision of femininity and sexuality before her.

"No, I'm just confused how this happened to you," Greta tried to explain. But how could she explain making a wish on a shooting star and then Angie turning into a bimbo? And how could she explain it in terms that a bimbo like Angie could understand.

"I've, like, always been this way, haven't I?" Angie asked. Even if it had not been a question, the way the pitch of her voice rose at the end made it clear that Angie was not sure. She needed Greta to confirm her already shaky memories.

"Last time I saw you, you were a single woman looking for a job," Greta explained. "You were plain and a bit nerdy. But I felt bad for you, so I wished that you would have a perfect life when I saw a shooting star last night. I didn't expect you to turn into some kind of bimbo. I just wanted you to maybe meet a nice guy and get a good job."

"But, like, I totally have a perfect life," Angie countered in her naturally sing-song voice. "I'm pretty and sexy and I'm totally horny, like, all the time. And guys pay me to hang out with them or they buy me stuff. I don't have to, like, think at all, except about how sexy I am and what sexy outfits and shoes I want to wear. I'm totally happy and love my perfect life. I just wish you could be like me, because if you're gonna be a mean bitch to me, I'm totally going to stop being your friend anymore. I may be a dumb bimbo, but I don't have to take your stupid shit, Greta."

Unbeknownst to both women, there was still some wish magic left over from Angie's transformation. In a flash of pink, Greta transformed right there in the cafe. Where before she had been wearing a loose sweater and a long, flowing skirt, her outfit had become a slutty clubbing dress with a deep cowl neck that went all the way to her belly-button. Her body shrunk and expanded in a similar way to Angie. Greta's tits grew large and round, although they were slightly smaller than Angie's, the magic of the wish running out before they could grow to an equal size.

But everything else about the two women was mostly equal. They were both ultra-feminine bimbos, inside and out. And where once Greta held down a normal job, now she worked as a slutty secretary for a sleazy lawyer who always made it a point to fuck her throughout the day. Not that Greta was complaining. She now saw that as a benefit of her job. And she got to fuck the clients too. It was the best of all worlds in her now bimbofied mind.

"O-M-G," Greta cooed. "Did I just turn into a bimbo too?"

"Um," Angie said, trying to think. Her memory was bad as it was, but she had been sitting there when it all happened. "I, like, think so."

"That's totally hot," Greta gushed. "But, like, why are we here at this boring cafe? Let's go find someplace fun where we can pick up guys. I'm horny."

"Ooh, that's totally a good idea," Angie agreed. "I'm horny too."

The two bimbos left the cafe, making a big scene with their sexy bodies on display in their sexy dresses, their high heels clicking and clacking on the hard floor, making sure that everyone saw them make their exit. Neither woman had expected to turn into a bimbo when all of this started. It was a wish on a shooting star that had gone awry. But now that Angie and Greta were bimbos, they could not imagine a more perfect life for themselves. They were happy and sexy and horny and that was all that mattered to them now.

FASHION STUDIES

"This is dumb," Monica told her professor after her first Fashion Studies class. She was taking the course as an elective, figuring she might learn something she could use when she graduated college and entered the professional world. Monica was not someone who was naturally trendy, but if she could learn the trends, she could make sure she always looked fashionable enough to get by, especially in a world where looking good at her job meant almost as much as being good at her job.

However, that was not what Monica was going to be learning in Fashion Studies. No, it seemed the class was being provided for all the bimbos in the student body who just wanted to gossip and learn how to pair their makeup and jewelry to their outfits.

In all her time at Thatcher College, Monica had never seen so many obvious bimbos all at once. She knew the school seemed to cater to dumb and sexy women in some strange way that was never fully understood by her, but they mostly stayed out of her way. That was until now. Now Monica found herself surrounded by them in what was supposed to be a fluff course that would pay dividends in the future.

Worse, there was the professor. Monica did not even believe the woman who called herself Professor Titz—that was her real last name—was an actual member of the faculty. She looked like someone the Dean had possibly picked up at the strip club. Her full name was actually Candi Titz. Given the fitted pink dress suit she wore to class, complete with matching high heels, Professor Titz was trying to look professional, but in a way that screamed bimbo. She was not even wearing a blouse beneath the suit jacket. Her big, round tits were on complete display, her nipples always threatening to peak out if she raised her shoulders too much.

"What's your name again?" Professor Titz asked as she confronted Monica. Her voice was high pitched and soft, making her sound weak and submissive. It gave the impression that someone could steam roll right over her. However, Professor Titz was a full tenure track member of the faculty. There was little that Monica could do or say that would hurt the professor, no matter what Monica decided to share with the school administration.

"Monica Reynolds. But you don't need to bother learning it. I'll be dropping your class. I thought I might actually learn something, but the moment I saw you walk into the classroom, I knew it was pointless. There is literally nothing you can teach me. Now if you'll excuse me, I need to go prepare for a real class."

"Hold on a moment, Miss Reynolds," Professor Titz said. She placed a hand on Monica's shoulder and the young woman suddenly froze, unable to move.

Panic began to well up inside of Monica. She had never felt so helpless before. Her body was not responding to her brain. She could still breathe and she could still blink, but she could not even open her mouth to try and scream. Every voluntary movement she could make had just been made impossible.

"Yes, I have frozen you in place," Professor Titz explained. Her voice was still soft and high pitched, but there was a seriousness in it to make it clear that she meant business. "I will not accept the derision you have placed on my class, my teaching methods, or myself. Therefore, I am using my powers as a member of the Thatcher College faculty to rectify your behavior."

Even for Monica, who considered herself to be a smart and capable student, those were a lot of big words that made the professor harder to understand. But while some of those words might have gone over Monica's head, the meaning behind them was clear. Monica had overstepped her bounds and now she was going to be punished for it. The only question was what punishment Professor Titz had in mind for her. Monica had never been in trouble with a teacher before, so this was completely new territory for her and the fact Professor Titz was devising her punishment made it all the worse.

"You can tell me that you understand and that you will submit for your punishment," Professor Titz added.

Monica suddenly felt her jaw relax. Her ability to speak had been returned to her, although the rest of her body remained frozen.

"I understand and will submit for my punishment," Monica said, her voice coming out surprisingly flat, almost like she had been robotically compelled to speak. However, that was not the case. It was her decision to speak. It was just that she did not know what else she could say. She did not want to make her punishment worse than it already was.

Monica was aware that punishing students at Thatcher College was rare. Students would get warnings and that was usually all that was required. The other students did not push the boundaries of what was allowed, or so she had seen. If there were more severe punishments, she had not known anyone who experienced them.

But that was what made this all the weirder. Never mind the fact that Professor Titz had somehow managed to freeze Monica in place by just placing a hand on her shoulder. That would take more than a little analyzing to figure out how it was done. It almost felt as if there was some sort of electrical charge flowing into her that froze her muscles, but that did not explain how it could be so specific and how Professor Titz seemed able to control what part of her froze.

"Good," Professor Titz said as she lifted her hand from Monica's shoulder. "Come to my office this evening, let's say at seven. I'm sure we will have all of this figured out by the end of tonight."

"Yes, Professor," Monica said, her voice returning to normal now that she was free of her professor's influence.

As soon as it was clear to do so, Monica dashed out of the classroom and away from her professor before any minds could be changed. She did not want to spend any more time with Professor Titz than she had to. And knowing she now needed to spend her evening with the woman made it all worse. Monica felt as if she had been assigned detention. She had never gotten detention before in her life. And she had assumed the possibility of detention had been removed once she started college. It seemed she had assumed wrongly.

Monica did her best to put the thought of her meeting with Professor Titz out of her mind. However, even as she went about her day, adjusting to her new class schedule, the prospect of meeting with her professor that evening weighed on the back of her mind. It definitely sucked the fun out of what would have been an otherwise good day.

Monica waved goodbye to her friends as she left the dining hall. It had been a good chance to catch up with her friends after the break. Monica elected not to share the fact that she was being reprimanded by one of her professors. However, as soon as she was done with her punishment, Monica planned to drop the class and replace it with something more academically challenging. Her desire to learn about how to dress for success in the business world would have to wait for another opportunity. Maybe the yearly etiquette dinner would provide some of what she needed.

Monica had to look up where Professor Titz's office was, because it was not located in any of the usual academic buildings. Her office was a block off campus in a building that had formerly been a funeral parlor. Monica did not want to imagine the stories that the walls of the building could tell if able, but she understood that sometimes a college needed to expand into whatever spaces were available.

Walking up to the building, Monica could not immediately tell that the building had previously been a funeral parlor. Although there was a large side door that was more than likely the door that bodies were brought in through. But that was not the door Monica went in. She used the front door of the building.

From there, it was actually easy to find her professor's office. It was the only office door that was open. All of the other doors were shut, without even a light showing from underneath. Most professors did not work this late unless they were teaching a night class and those classes had generally already started. There was no reason for any of them to be in their offices. Only Professor Titz had a reason to be present.

The door was open, but Monica still knocked on the doorframe as she stepped into the doorway. Professor Titz was sitting behind her desk, looking at her phone. She looked up and smiled. However, the smile Professor Titz gave was not the sort that made Monica feel welcome. It was a predatory smile. It was a smile that told Monica she was going to be in for quite a night, whatever that meant.

"You're on time," Professor Titz said. "I like to see that. But don't think that being on time will win you any points, Miss Reynolds, because your words earlier today were a clear signal that you don't respect me or the course you signed up for. But I'm sure by the time tonight is over, you will see things a little differently. Take a seat and we'll get started."

Professor Tits motioned toward a chair in front of the desk. Monica entered the office quickly and sat down as beckoned. Her heart raced in her chest, the blood pounding in her ears. She had never been in trouble like this before. It scared her, now more than ever, especially with the way the professor had looked at her.

Standing up, Professor Titz walked around the desk. As she did so, she turned her computer monitor so that it faced Monica instead of where she had just been sitting. Then Professor Titz closed the office door, cutting off Monica's only escape route. Not that the young woman expected to need to escape. Although if she understood what her professor had in store for her, she might have wanted to escape before it was too late.

"It's clear to me that we need to change your mind about a few things," Professor Titz said. She had changed her top so that she now wore a soft sweater with a large boob window cut out of it. Just as before, her nipples were just barely kept hidden from view. The sweater had been paired with a short skirt that hugged her impressive backside wonderfully. Just as with her outfit during class, Professor Titz looked more like a bimbo professor than an actual academic. She looked like she was cosplaying as a professor when she was really a stripper or other sex worker.

The monitor flickered on and Monica found herself

looking at an image of herself. At least it looked a lot like Monica. It was a near perfect computer generated avatar of her. The background was some sort of multicolored spiral, but the whole image was static.

"It's time to learn your place," Professor Titz said. As soon as she said those words, the image came to life. The avatar on the screen started to move ever so slightly, much like a real person would when they stood up. But the real movement came as the spiral started to spin. Monica immediately found her eyes locked onto the screen, unable to look away.

And a moment later, the computer speakers began to play some sort of strange static sound. As soon as Monica's brain registered the sound, it was like the whole world went flat. The only thing that made sense was the spiral and the image of Monica on the screen. Everything else was removed from existence.

It was a strange sensation to have her entire mind just stop working. One moment she was ready to roll her eyes at whatever form of punishment this was and the next she drew an entire blank. Monica would not have even been able to recall her name in her current state. All thought patterns had ceased. The only parts of her brain that still worked were those that handled involuntary functions like breathing and keeping her heart pumping. Everything else had stopped.

"Welcome to your re-education, Monica," Professor Titz said. Her voice came through the speakers and sounded oddly distorted with the static, but Monica understood her words perfectly. It was almost like they were being drilled into her head. "You have been deluded into believing that you are an intelligent and independent woman. It is time that you embrace your true self. It is time that you finally discover what it means to truly be happy."

With no thoughts to push back against the professor's

words, Monica could not help to agree with them. They became a new truth that she simply could not argue against.

"There was a reason you signed up for Fashion Studies," Professor Titz continued. "You want to be fashionable. You know that a woman like yourself doesn't have the ability to succeed in the wide world. You are weak and dumb. Therefore you need to focus on your best assets. That means you want to look as good as you can. You need to highlight your body so that no one cares about what happens in your head."

Deep down, Monica knew that none of what Professor Titz said was true, but without the means to counter her arguments, all she could do was accept them. The static pouring out of the speakers and the spiral spinning on the screen had eliminated all of what made Monica herself. All she could do was mindlessly agree with her professor's words, accepting them as truth.

"Your past self is an illusion. The idea of being a successful college student was simply good luck. You've always known that you were not smart enough for the academic rigor of college. That's why you chose to attend Thatcher College. You knew that there were programs here that you could understand and that would help you live a full life. So now you are here. You have joined my Fashion Studies course. You finally realize that all of those other classes were too hard for you. Any good grades you received were just good luck. Your strengths lie elsewhere and now you're going to embrace your true self."

Professor Titz went on for what could have been hours or merely minutes. All Monica knew was that every word her professor spoke was the truth. Her memories were still her own, but now she understood that those memories were fleeting grasps at a normal life. Monica was not made for a normal life. She was far too simple for that. She needed constant guidance. Her mind was like a sieve, retaining only the simplest of information. Anything she thought she knew before was probably wrong.

And yet, as all of these new truths sunk in for the first time, Monica found her happiness rising. She no longer had to hide. She no longer had to pretend. She could be the dumb and pretty woman she was always meant to be. She was freed of the trouble of her past and could now embrace her true purpose in life. And chief among her new desires was pleasing men.

Monica smiled as the session with Professor Titz ended. She looked up at her professor and admired how pretty she looked. She looked down at her own body and understood that she had potential, but she was still a long way off from being as pretty as her professor. Monica would need to workout hard to make her body toned and fit. She might need surgery to give her big, round boobies too. But she knew all of that sacrifice would be worth it, because men liked women with big tits and small brains. And that was going to be Monica. She was going to be the best bimbo she could be.

The next day, Monica visited her adviser as she had originally planned. However, rather than drop Fashion Studies, Monica moved to completely change her major. Fashion Studies would simply become the foundation upon which she would build her new life. There was Home Ec, Relationship Studies, and even Sex Ed. Monica was starting with a blank slate, but between Professor Titz and her advisor, she quickly righted the wrongs she had made in her past.

Monica's friends did not understand her sudden change in attitude. They were flabbergasted that Monica now called herself dumb and how she explained that she needed to emphasize what she was best at, which was being pretty and pleasing men. However, rather than support their friend, they instead pulled away, cutting Monica out of the friend group. That worked out just fine for Monica. She made new friends in her new classes, befriending the bimbos on campus and allowing them to help her be the best bimbo she could be.

By the end of the semester, Monica was acing all of her classes. Her boob job had gone off without a hitch and she could not be happier as a slutty bimbo. Her start in some of her new classes had been rough, especially Sex Ed. It turned out that even though Monica had sex before, she really did not know what she was doing before. By focusing on his pleasure, her pleasure became magnified almost ten-fold. She had no idea, but now a day when she was not getting her brains fucked out was a rare day. It all felt so good.

But the best part about all of it, once Monica had finished her Bimbo Studies degree, was that she was paired up with a man who would serve as her master. The moment Monica laid eyes on her intended owner, she was in love. She could not wait to become his, pleasing him with her body in exchange for him taking care of her needs. Monica could not imagine a better life. She was a bimbo through and through and she had Professor Titz to thank for it all. She had seen Monica's potential and made sure that she got to live her best bimbo life.

BIMBO POPS

Kizzy thought Bimbo Pops were a joke. The special popsicle was just a gag she would eat on a hot day. Nothing real would come from it. It was just a funny way of naming a pink popsicle that was flavored like cotton candy.

But Bimbo Pops were no joke. And Kizzy had purchased the extra strength Bimbo Pops. They tasted exactly the same as normal strength Bimbo Pops, but instead of having just temporary effects, these ones were permanent.

"Yum," Kizzy said after her first lick. It was like eating frozen cotton candy, which was perfect when the temperature had her sweating the moment she stepped outside.

However, the moment Kizzy pushed the Bimbo Pop into her mouth, having only licked it previously, she found herself shoving it all the way in, pushing into her throat. Kizzy had never given a blowjob before, but that was where her mind immediately went. Her lips were wrapped around the base of the popsicle, much like she imagined her lips would be wrapped around the base of a cock. The only significant difference was the temperature. The Bimbo Pop was frozen and a cock would presumably be warm.

It only took a moment with the popsicle lodged in Kizzy's throat for the effects of the Bimbo Pop to start. Kizzy started feeling lightheaded. It was not from a lack of blood flow or other normal form of lightheadedness. It was a sensation she experienced as her normal thoughts began to slip away. It was a lightness caused by the disappearance of her concerns and worries. The fact that Kizzy's rent check was due next week and that she wanted to make sure she had enough money in her bank account to cover the check completely slipped her mind.

Kizzy would have smiled except the Bimbo Pop was still in her mouth, slowly melting as her head became filled with cotton candy. Only sweet thoughts were making it through the web of saccharine happiness that surrounded her mind. Sadness, anger, and all manner of negative emotions could not make it through the candy filter.

But as the Bimbo Pop melted and the juices slowly worked their way into Kizzy's body, the physical transformation effects began as well. Kizzy, despite her name, had looked more gothic than bimbo. She wore dark clothing and her skin remained pale from her many hours spent indoors, often in a library reading what would have otherwise been depressing literature. Her name was a complete misnomer, because she was not light or airy as her name might imply. Her attitude was normally dark and brooding, with a solid sense of irony.

That was half the reason Kizzy had selected the Bimbo Pop to help her cool down on such a hot day. She had done so for the irony, because she would be the last person someone would expect to be a bimbo. Yes, Kizzy liked the cotton candy flavor, but she would never allow herself to be seen eating such a delicious treat. Kizzy had a reputation to uphold.

However, as her body absorbed the melted popsicle, it

began to change. It started with Kizzy's skin. Her almost sickly pale skin began to darken, gaining a tan that only someone who spent hours each week sunning themselves could achieve or they regularly received a high level spray tan that avoided the orange look. Only her face was visible as her dark clothing covered the rest of her body, but Kizzy had gained a perfect and complete tan, without a single tan line anywhere on her body.

Next came a general tightening and toning of her body. Kizzy was already relatively fit, at least for the activities that she participated in, which included long walks through creepy forests or even through graveyards at night, but there was always room for improvement. Her musculature shifted and strengthened, giving her a tight and toned body that was worth showing off instead of hiding behind layers of thick, dark clothing.

Not that Kizzy understood any of this. She did not even feel her body changing. She had no concept it was happening, because her mind was still under the onslaught of the Bimbo Pop. But if she could see herself in a mirror or even if she was able to just look down and see her new body, she would have found joy in it. Her thoughts would have revolved around how sexy she looked now without worry of how or why her body had changed. With the Bimbo Pop, such considerations were no longer regarded as important.

Heat suffused her body. Her body had started to change, but for the next part in her transformation, Kizzy needed to remove her clothes. Otherwise the growth she was about to experience would cause her great pain.

With the Bimbo Pop still in her mouth, Kizzy began to tear at her clothing. She could not stop herself from ripping off her dark clothes, using both hands to remove every scrap. She needed to be naked. That was the only way that she could finally release all the heat that had built up inside her body.

And once Kizzy was naked, she let out a long moan with the relief of finally being able to cool down. Had she been able to consider her predicament, she would have realized that the heat she felt could not have been real while she had the Bimbo Pop in her mouth. It was a minor miracle that she was not experiencing brain freeze. Then again, Kizzy's brain had gone through massive changes and there was not much there to "freeze".

But Kizzy's nudity provided the needed space for her body to get the upgrades that would forever more label her a bimbo. It started in her chest. Kizzy's hands automatically shot up to her breasts as she felt a pressure building up inside of them. She could only stand there and watch as her breasts expanded into her hands, growing large and round until they stuck off her body with incredible projection, becoming a proper pair of bimbo tits.

The growth was too much for Kizzy's bimbofied mind to comprehend. All she knew was that she loved her tits. They felt good. They felt, in bimbo-speak, yummy. Her hard nipples squeezed through the gaps between her fingers, the added friction sending a shockwave of pleasure through her body, both hitting her brain and her pussy at the same time.

Kizzy finally released her tits and pulled the Bimbo Pop from between her lips so that she could take a much needed breath. As her lungs filled with more air, her tits took on one last growth spurt.

"Wow," Kizzy said as she looked down into her cleavage. Thoughts of a big cock sliding between her tits now dominated her mind. It seemed like such a natural thing and she seemed certain that it would feel good, especially when that cock spurt all that cum over her chest.

However, while Kizzy was busy imagining her tits getting

fucked by a cock, her ass was expanding an almost equal amount. Where once she had been flat and generally ignored, now her butt was growing out into a perfect bubble. There would always be questions about whether or not her ass was real. The answer was that it did not matter. All that mattered was that it looked fantastic. Between her tits and her ass, people would always have something hot to look at when Kizzy was near.

But it was not just her tits and ass that expanded. It was her lips too, both on her face and between her legs. As Kizzy began to suck on the Bimbo Pop anew, her lips expanded around it, gaining volume and projection. By the time they finished growing, Kizzy could look down her nose and see her lips push into the lower part of her vision, much like her tits did too.

Down between her thighs, however, there was a different kind of growth. There her pussy lips grew plump and fleshy. Her clit grew in size as well, throwing back its hood and asserting its dominance when it came to sex. Forevermore, the lightest touch would be enough to turn Kizzy on. Even the most inept lover would be sure to get her off. Kizzy's body had already been redesigned for sex. Her body would crave it, her libido kicked up into overdrive.

As Kizzy finished the Bimbo Pop, getting down to the stick at its center, Kizzy felt as if she was on top of the world. Her mind was in the clouds, her body was aching for sex, and there was nothing that could get her down. Kizzy was happy. As a recently created bimbo, she could be nothing else. Happiness was her default attitude. That and horny. Kizzy's pussy glistened with her juices as she spread her legs. She was not at the point of leaking, but if she did get off soon, she soon would be.

"That was, like, the best popsicle ever," Kizzy explained as she licked the stick clean. She sucked on the stick for a little while, her brain fizzing with pleasurable nothingness. It was like bubbles popped in her head, releasing any remaining thoughts into the ether. It was a wonderful experience.

Once Kizzy finished her Bimbo Pop completely, finally throwing away the stick, her mind immediately turned toward sex. She needed it badly. And if she did not find a willing partner soon, it would be up to her to take care of her own needs. It was not that Kizzy was against masturbation. She loved it, especially now, but a willing partner made it so much better.

Kizzy looked out the window of her apartment. She had never bothered to close her blinds. Anyone could have seen her transformation into a bimbo goddess. They could see her now in all her bimbo glory. It looked hot outside. The sun still beat down out there. The people on the street, none of whom were looking in through the window at Kizzy, looked hot, even wearing shorts and T-shirts, sweat on their brows. Kizzy was hot too, but while she was sexy and turned on beyond belief, she did not feel the high temperature that the others did.

However, as Kizzy looked out the window, she saw her neighbor walk up toward the apartment complex. She had never given him the time of day before, even though he had asked her out several times. His name was Lee, but Kizzy could not remember it now. She did not care about names. She just knew that he had a cock.

Never bothering to put clothes on—it was doubtful any would fit her now, at least in a way that she would want to wear them—Kizzy burst out of her apartment just as Lee was walking by toward his own front door. She grabbed him and pushed him up against the wall, planting her plump lips against his and kissing him with all of her might.

Lee was shocked to start, but as soon as he realized that he was getting kissed by an amazingly sexy and naked woman, he started to kiss her back. He dropped his bag to the ground, no longer caring about its contents. His hands reached up and began to explore Kizzy's curves. It was unlike anything he had ever experienced before. Lee was an attractive man, but he had still struggled with women. Now he had the sexiest woman he had ever seen throwing herself at him in a fit of passion that he could never have dreamed of before.

It was not long before Kizzy pulled Lee into her apartment. It was only once they were inside that Lee had any idea of who this woman might be.

"Kizzy?" he asked, confused. But it looked like her, although he had never thought she was this busty before. Not that Lee was complaining.

"Of course, stud," Kizzy cooed. "Now fuck me like a bimbo. Fuck my brains out."

Lee could have commented that she did not sound like she had any brains left. That was true, at least compared to the old Kizzy. But that was not going to stop Lee now. He was not about to ignore a bimbo that had fallen into his lap demanding that he fuck her.

It only took a moment before his shorts were on the floor. The rest of his clothes soon followed. His cock stood at attention, having never been harder before. Kizzy's eyes locked onto his cock and she drooled from both sets of lips.

Kizzy positioned herself on the couch, pushing her ass out at Lee. It was clear what she wanted. He could see the arousal in her eyes as she looked at him over her shoulder. Her body was sexual perfection. And as Lee stepped up behind her, he placed his hands on her hips. It felt as if his hands were meant to be there. A moment later he thrust his cock into her pussy. He did not need to take it slow. He rammed himself all the way in for the first time, his hips meeting her expanded backside.

"Fuck yes," Kizzy screamed out as her eyes rolled up into the back of her head. Already the pleasure was overwhelming her. Lee might have been inexperienced, but he was not unskilled and he had a cock that pushed all of her buttons.

Lee could not believe his luck. He fucked Kizzy hard, treating her body as a sex doll made for his pleasure. But the more he focused on his pleasure, it seemed as if Kizzy's body responded with greater cries of pleasure. But all of that paled in comparison to when she finally came. Her orgasm exploded inside of her when Lee finally shot his load into her. Wave after wave of orgasmic pleasure cascaded through her body. Her limbs convulsed as almost everything shut down in response, only her heart and lungs still working.

"I think I really did fuck your brains out," Lee said as he stood up. Kizzy had collapsed onto the couch, her face planted into the cushions and her ass still sticking up into the air.

"Totally," she mumbled into the couch.

Lee did not know what to do. He did not feel that it was safe to leave Kizzy in her current situation, so he wandered around her apartment, trying to get an idea of what had happened to her while she recovered.

"Bimbo Pops," Lee read as he found the wrapper for the Bimbo Pop she had eaten earlier. "Extra Strength."

While Lee had not had much experience with women, he knew all about Bimbo Pops. He wondered if Kizzy had meant to eat one and if she had meant to turn into the bimbo she now was. Not that it mattered.

"Kizzy, baby," Lee said as he decided to take action. "Let's get you up so you can come over to my apartment. You're going to live with me from now on."

Kizzy managed to look at Lee and smile. That sounded wonderful. Living with Lee would mean more access to his cock. And while he had fucked her already, she had two more holes for him to try. It seemed like a huge win for her.

Kizzy might have been curious to try a Bimbo Pop before, but now she was unable to imagine another way of life. And since she had accidentally bought an extra strength Bimbo Pop, she was a bimbo now. It was permanent. Kizzy was finally living up to her name. Ditzy Kizzy was embarking on a new adventure that was sure to come with lots of orgasms and endless happiness. She was no longer on the goth spectrum. She was a bimbo now through and through.

ABOUT THE AUTHOR

Sadie Thatcher is a longtime author of erotic fiction, especially related to transformations and bimbofication. She likes to say "I have thrown off the shackles of my conservative upbringing and now write erotic stories."

She maintains a special blog devoted to her writings, including a behind the scenes look at her writing process, and bimbos in general, as well as highlights works by other authors. They can be found at:

https://authorsadiethatcher.tumblr.com

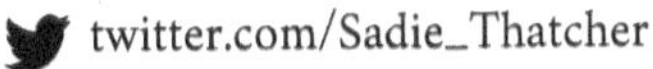 twitter.com/Sadie_Thatcher

The Bimbo Professor: The Curse of Playing Bimbo Tag Book 3

Anything for the Job

Anything for the Job 2

Anything for His Job

The Bimbo in the Mirror

The Bimbo in the Mirror 2

Astrid and the Bimbo Bee

Bella and the Bimbo Bee

Cali and the Bimbo Bee

Desiree and the Bimbo Bee

Ember and the Bimbo Bee

Fiona and the Bimbo Bee

The Intern

The Lawyer

The Hacker

Cause & Effect

Witless Protection

Stealing Sally

Trial and Error

Beta Testing

Exposed

Bimbo for a Weekend

Bimbo for a Week

Bimbo for Life

Surprise!

Fake It Until You Make It Season 1

Fake It Until You Make It Season 2

Fake It Until You Make It Season 3

Simple and Fun Volume 1

Simple and Fun Volume 2

Simple and Fun Volume 3

Simple and Fun Volume 4

Simple and Fun Volume 5

Simple and Fun Volume 6

Silly Bimbo Volume 1

Silly Bimbo Volume 2

Bimbo Halloween

Bimbo Christmas

Bimbo Technology

Dorm Room Bimbo

Carissa's Magic Pen

Spirit Walk

Muscle Memory

The Case of the Bimbo Wife

Changes

Changes 2

New Year New You

The Bimbo Dream

The Wedding Gift

The Cure

Backfire

Bim & Bo Yoga

Wishing for Each Other

Bimbo Roots

A Bimbo at Oktoberfest

The Lost Bet

Milk and Bliss

The Fighter

The Help

The Bimbo Resort

Awakening

Body Swap Rings: Happy Anniversary

Body Swap Rings 2: Wedding Night

The Bimbo Experience

The Bimbo Experience 2

The Bimbo Experience 3some

The 4th Bimbo Experience

Bimbo Genes

Bimbo Genes II: The Virus

The Bimbo Genes III: The Epidemic

Bimbo Juice: Blue Raspberry

Bimbo Juice: Grape

Bimbo Juice: Mango

Bimbo Juice: Pineapple

Bimbo Juice: Red Apple

Bimbo Juice: Veggie

Bimbo Juice Gone Wild: The Muse

Bimbo Juice Gone Wild: Street Racer

Bimbo Juice Gone Wild: Score

Bimbos of the Traveling Earrings: Book 1

Bimbos of the Traveling Earrings: Book 2

Bimbos of the Traveling Earrings: Book 3

Bimbos of the Traveling Earrings: Book 4

Bimbo Party: Kennedy